Forgiveness

Forgiveness

Gillian Stokes

Red Wheel
Boston, MA / York Beach, ME

First published by MQ Publications Limited, 12 The Ivories, 6–8
Northhampton St., London, N1 2HY

First published in the United States in 2002 by
Red Wheel/Weiser, LLC
York Beach, ME
With editorial offices at:
368 Congress Street
Boston, MA 02210
www.redwheelweiser.com

ISBN: 1-59003-036-2

Printed in China

09 08 07 06 05 04 03 02
9 8 7 6 5 4 3 2 1

The paper used in this publication meets the minimum requirements of
the American National Standard for Information Sciences—
Permanence of Paper for Printed Library Materials Z39.48-1992 (R1997).

Permissions have been sought where possible for all quotations used.
Please contact the company for any information regarding these.

Contents

Preface

❝ *...true forgiveness is a self-healing process which starts with you and gradually extends to everyone else.* **❞**

ROBERT HOLDEN

The question of forgiveness or blame may only become personal after a major loss or disappointment, when strong feelings can become self-destructive. But what if you were equipped with a better way to respond? What if, instead of living in anger, you chose to forgive? That is no simple task. Forgiving is a skill that few of us come by naturally; most of us have to learn it, and we all have to practice at it.

66 *Forgiveness: To stop feeling angry or resentful towards someone for an offence, flaw, or mistake.* 99

THE NEW OXFORD ENGLISH DICTIONARY, 1998

As with most skills, forgiveness requires commitment and effort. It can take many years and take us through several stages. But don't save forgiveness for the big transgressions, to grudgingly bestow at great sacrifice. Forgiveness is a life skill to use daily—in small ways as well as large. For example, strive to forgive the person who pushes into line ahead of you and the one whose slow driving will make you late for work. Forgive the rudeness from the coworker who doesn't seem to know better. Forgive the salesgirl who shortchanged you; she must have really needed your money to have risked her job.

Have you ever raged at someone because you felt angry at an entirely different person? Such petty aggravations can play havoc with your health and your relationships. But, remember, you have the choice of treating each experience as a chance to fuel the fire of your rage or as an opportunity to practice forgiveness. Used daily, forgiveness can bring harmony to your life. Your digestion and sleep patterns will benefit as less adrenaline courses through your body, and you will stop wasting your precious energy. Let the Divine sort out whether retribution is due.

This book offers no quick fixes: Forgiving is a process, sometimes a long one. As we move toward complete forgiveness, we will look at advice given by many philosophies and religions. If you decide not to forgive in a certain situation, I hope to encourage you to discover why and to explore other options that might improve your life.

> Holding on to anger is like grasping a hot coal with the intent of throwing it at someone else; you are the one who gets burned.
>
> BUDDHA

What Is Forgiveness?

66 …*whosoever believeth in Him shall receive forgiveness of sins.* 99

THE HOLY BIBLE, ACTS 10:43

Forgiveness is both a religious and a psychological issue. Regardless of their faith, or lack of it, most members of Western society see forgiveness as a spiritual or noble act. It certainly sits at the heart of Christian theology—Christians believe that Jesus died to redeem (or forgive) our sins and that He forgave His persecutors while in agony on the cross. This Christian example set a precedent for Western moral behavior and is, inevitably, a very hard act to follow.

Whatever our own religious persuasion, we may feel pressured to follow this self-sacrificing example and forgive those who have acted dishonorably, when, in reality, we may feel more inclined to murderous retaliation. Our inability to easily forgive can add a further burden of guilt and shame.

Psychotherapists tread more cautiously than the Christian church and make no global recommendations regarding forgiveness, suggesting instead that each case proceed according to the history and ability of the individual involved. In certain circumstances, attempting forgiveness might be ill-advised. Listen to your instinct and seek professional advice if your wounds and their re-examination seem too overwhelming to handle alone. Seek out the support of a friend, family member, or church official—someone you trust completely—to help you in this process.

So, what do I mean by *forgiveness*? First let's examine what it is not. In forgiving, we do not endorse what happened, nor do we pretend that any resulting consequences were not deserved. If the wrongdoers have been caught and punished, they have merely experienced the legal

> ❝ *It is easier to forgive an enemy than to forgive a friend.* ❞

WILLIAM BLAKE

result of their actions. Forgiveness is not about law reform, though in a case of injustice, it could become one. Forgiveness is not about ignoring the pain we feel. Forgiveness is definitely not about permitting ourselves to get hurt again. As adults, we must take responsibility for our own emotional and physical safety. Children and animals have the right to expect us to guard their safety.

Forgiveness *is* a choice. We choose to change our thoughts, beliefs, and ideas about a situation or person. We must decide to let go of the negative emotions that the experience evokes. Through forgiveness, we can reclaim personal peace and tranquillity. Though the memories may still hurt, we refuse to let them dominate us.

Therefore, I encourage you to see the benefits of forgiving. However, forgiveness may not be right for every person, every situation, or every moment. Regardless of our moral or religious upbringing—those calls that we've heard throughout life to forgive and forget, turn the other cheek, love the sinner and hate the sin—we may face situations where well-controlled, righteous anger are both justified and necessary for our psychological health and physical safety. However, you should continue to work toward calmer states, when forgiveness can become a viable, renewed option. In the end, we suffer more than the focus of our hatred. In some instances, we may have to live with the impossibility of

❝No one can make you feel inferior without your consent.❞

ELEANOR ROOSEVELT

giving, or getting, forgiveness. We will explore the possible implications of choosing not to forgive later in this book.

Whether we choose to forgive or not, we must take responsibility for our actions. We must not cause harm to others, especially when exacting revenge seems enticing. Such action would merely take us deeper in our pain—we would have to bear the additional burden of having acted out of character. We'd also have to live with the knowledge and guilt that, under pressure, we respond as badly as those who hurt us. Scores do not get evened by retaliation; they double.

There are positive ways to live with pain and anger when we cannot forgive, ways to limit the debilitating effects of living with rage. These emotions can even provide a resource for fueling peaceful endeavors. We will explore some of these valid options. The exact methods you choose for forgiving, or for living with not forgiving, will be those that best suit your temperament. There is no strict formula. We must handle each of our experiences according to its unique nature and approach the question of forgiveness with sensitivity, self-awareness, and responsibility for ourselves and others.

Perfection

❝Do not reproach another for a blemish that is in you.❞
RASHI

You are not required to be perfect because nothing and no one in the universe is. Do not try to take on that impossible burden as you tackle your feelings of rage or regret. Try not to expect perfection in others because they will disappoint you. Even the Christian Saints had their flaws. Saint Augustine, a priest and towering figure in medieval philosophy who was no stranger to worldly desires commented in his text *Confessions*: *"Give me chastity Lord and continence... but not today."*

Saint Augustine was well aware of his frailties and knew that he had a strong sexual appetite and that to pretend otherwise would be less than heartfelt living.

Leave perfection for the Divine, in whatever manifestation She or He adopts for you. Be true to yourself. All any of us can hope for is self-improvement. Do not despair or feel wicked if you feel rage or are unable to forgive someone who has wronged you. Few people can immediately and sincerely forgive another. Most of us have to work at it, to reason our way to a more comfortable attitude that can genuinely accommodate forgiveness. While forgiving does get easier with practice, those who forgive as a reflex action are either saintly, less than totally honest about their feelings, or not in touch with their feelings at all.

> 66 *The man with insight enough to admit his limitations comes nearest to perfection.* 99
>
> JOHANN VON GOETHE

Acknowledge Wrongdoing

" *To understand all is to forgive all.* "

MME DE STAËL 1766–1817

Since perfection is not an option this side of heaven, don't keep punishing yourself, or others, for past lapses or errors of judgment. The energy that you spend in maintaining your negative emotions—anger, hatred, or self-loathing—cannot change the truth of what happened. However, holding onto the pain, embarrassment, or anger continually causes you to revisit the past and infects the present. In despair, we lose hope and the willingness to trust. The pervasive cynicism that follows belittles every good thing. This bottled rage can ruin today and tomorrow, just as it ruined yesterday, to no good purpose. The longer you allow negative feelings to fester, the harder they become to eradicate—though not impossible. Keep in mind that appearing to forgive is not the same as genuinely forgiving from the heart, and only the latter can transform harmful negativity. The first step on the true path is to examine your feelings. What you cannot contemplate, you cannot forgive, and what you cannot forgive, you cannot overcome—we must begin by honestly acknowledging what happened.

This may sound foolish. Of course you know what happened. However, there is a world of difference between knowing the historical facts, and admitting what you felt then, and feel now, and why you reacted as you did. Rarely does the act itself so upset us. What matter are the feelings that get stirred up.

If you have severe trauma in your past, this retrospective examination may seem too much to bear. Blocking off certain feelings may have been a survival skill—to endure the traumatic situation. And perhaps your feelings should remain blocked, at least until you spontaneously wish to re-examine them or you have a safe therapeutic environment in which to explore them. If you feel ready to evaluate your past, consider why you reacted in the way that you did. If you were hurt then you should reassess the nature of the hurt. Was it a lack or an absence—something you expected or hoped for but did not receive? Do you have strong childhood memories of this sort of experience that feel tied to the present? Do you need to start by forgiving an earlier individual or group before you approach those involved in a present event?

If you take a pain reliever for a toothache but ignore the rotten tooth, you can expect the pain to return. Examine how your current feelings have become entangled with your painful memories. Did you suffer an imposition against your will? Was it a snub or rejection that felt demeaning? Did you feel ashamed? Powerless? Reflect on what happened recently. Why did it trip the switch? Do you have old memories of feeling this way? Think about the quality of the hurt and whether similar provocation always touches a raw nerve. Perhaps you get upset when you encounter such a case in the media or in fiction—a book, film, or television program. For example, my mother died more than thirty years ago, but because of unresolved pain that needed to be

> ## *An injury is much sooner forgotten than an insult.*

LORD CHESTERFIELD

forgiven on both sides, I could not talk about her death for two or three years without bursting into tears. I could not bear to watch a televised funeral or read of a fictional death for very many more years after that. I even found some advertisements upsetting.

Perhaps the trauma you suffered left you with a huge, frightening reservoir of pain. Even though you know your inability to let it go is hurting you, you fear that if you let even a drop of it out, you might never gain control over it again. A giant wave might engulf you and everything in its path. But this is more likely to happen if you *do nothing*. A certain trigger on a certain day will cause the dam to burst—

66 *It is a man's own mind,*

not his enemy or foe

usually out of proportion to the trigger, and often to the amazement of those who witness it. Those who hold back their emotions, especially rage, can appear tranquil and placid until the wrong word or deed...then the flood waters wash over everything, indiscriminately. Catch yourself the next time your dam bursts and think back. Let your pain take you to its source. This is the "wounded healer" at work. Until and unless you work with the original source of your pain and anger, forgiving later hurts will not prevent future outbursts.

For less severe offences, you can make peace with your anger unaided, but first you must get acquainted. Make a mental note of what triggers your strong emotions. Can you find a pattern to what makes you see red? Is it because you feel ignored, disobeyed, disrespected, abused, taken for granted, manipulated, physically or mentally coerced, lied to,

that lures him to evil ways. **99**

BUDDHA

tricked, deceived, neglected, abandoned, or all of these? The nature of your trigger reflects the type of hurt that you experienced and bound up long ago. This kind of reflection can also be useful if you always feel angry but cannot pinpoint the source of your rage.

"Why rake over the past at all?" you may ask. There is something to be said for changing the channel or going out to a movie instead of revisiting old pain, especially when you know full well what you are avoiding or feel incapable of exploring it. It may seem easier to avoid remembering painful or embarrassing moments. However, if you still feel the negative effects of those events, you are already reliving them, over and over. You add to your feelings of anger, shame, fear, grief, or guilt with every backward glance. Something about what you fear today has the power to remind you of someone or something from the past that hurt you. Do you find it painful to watch certain scenes in films, television programs, even sketches in comedy shows? Do you avoid all references to a place or particular activity? Are you afraid of, or threatened by, certain things or circumstances—confined spaces, heights, horses, water, open curtains at night, people of a certain appearance (blonds, redheads, the obese or very thin, those in uniform or other identifiable clothing)? Why? Did a relative drown and leave you feeling guilty for surviving? Perhaps you hold on to guilt because you did not prevent an accident but feel you might have, or should have? Were you trapped in an elevator or deliberately locked in a closet or involved in a house fire? Were you regularly bullied or ignored by someone with a certain hair color? Was an abuser of a particular build or appearance? Did you miss the chance to make up with your father before he died? Whatever the painful memories, you either repeatedly live the hurt or spend a tremendous amount of mental energy to avoid remembering it. Until you really acknowledge what about those past events caused your anguish, you cannot free yourself from the negative feelings that get in the way of fully enjoying your present or future.

Failures or Negative Results?

❝ God forgive you, but I never can. ❞

QUEEN ELIZABETH I TO THE COUNTESS
OF NOTTINGHAM

Some religions suggest that forgiveness is laudable and imply that a wronged person who cannot or will not forgive is somehow guilty of a sin. Unfortunately there are few saints and angels among us and as mere mortals, we must acknowledge our feelings and experiences, even if they are honestly negative or vengeful. No one has the right to demand we deny the past and its effect on our present; such crass judgment denies real feelings to the benefit of no one.

Healing can only begin with honesty. Leave it to God to punish the wrongdoer—that is not our responsibility. We have not failed if our honest response is, "I cannot."

Let's explore that response. Do the negative emotions you hold onto serve you better than the ability to forgive might? Are your negative emotions likely to have any negative effect upon the person or people you feel deserve your revenge? At the end of the day, is your anger worthwhile? Does it make a difference to anyone but you? Are the personal costs and effort worth it? These considerations may be of greater relevance than our choice to forgive according to prescribed religious or social ideals.

Anger and hatred are exhausting to maintain, yet they do not hurt the person that they are directed toward at all. Clarissa Pinkola Estès, author of *Women Who Run With the Wolves* (1992) aptly describes the state of perpetual anger as, *"… speeding through life 'pedal to the metal'; trying to live a balanced life with the accelerator pressed all the way to the floor."*

Estès also uses the metaphor of unset bones from a childhood fracture to illustrate the consequences of overdue forgiveness. Imperfect healing can cause much wider physiological maladjustment: poor gait and posture, impaired use of a limb, a compromised immune system. The body will compensate, and though life will continue, the individual bears constant physical reminders of the break. Such compensation will become habitual and more difficult to fix years later than would the child's original fracture, had the bone been immediately set. Difficult to rectify, but not impossible, with will and effort.

Just so with the crusted-over pain and compensatory anger of an adult who, as a child, did not get immediate emotional healing. The learned habits of cynicism, bitterness, and suspicion, of pouring negativity on others' happiness, of deadening empathy, and of shunning joy can become ingrained in such a survivor. Only through re-examining the source of the pain—the original broken bone, if you will—can the mending begin. Some should not attempt this without professional help. For most of us, our wounds, though numerous, are of Band-Aid rather than body-cast proportions.

It is bondage, when the mind desires anything or grieves about anything, rejects or welcomes anything, feels angry or happy about anything. Liberation is attained when the mind does not desire or grieve or reject or accept or feel happy or angry. It is bondage when the mind is attached to any particular sense organ. It is liberation when the mind is not attached to any sense organ. When there is no 'I' there is liberation; when there is 'I' there is bondage. Considering this, refrain from accepting or rejecting anything.

KASHYAPA IN THE ASHTAKAVRA SAMHITA, VIII

❝ *Nothing is so strong as gentleness and nothing is so gentle as real strength.* **❞**

RALPH W. SOCKMAN

Control

"A kind word is like a spring day."

RUSSIAN PROVERB

ealing restores a sense of control. You are more likely to find compassion and generosity from a calm position of strength. Therefore, learning how to manage the anger caused by psychological pain can help to free you from the past and make forgiveness possible.

Years of pain and anguish can so tightly bind us to our anger that we do not know any other way to be, but that can change. You were not born raging, and the potential for happiness that you possessed when you came into this world remains, under all the defenses. The road that seems closed to you can be reopened. If the prospect of releasing your anger is too frightening to contemplate, consider letting go in a more measured and controlled fashion.

How is your anger triggered? This awareness will help you know where and how to put on the brakes. Are you patient while standing in line, for example, or do you find yourself seething when you must wait? Were you thwarted when you tried to expand your will as a child? Can you observe the bad driving of another driver without feeling personally slighted and resorting to road rage? Do you argue with the television or radio? Ask friends or relatives to tell you what they think annoys you. They will surely know; if they are still around, they have learned to avoid those topics. Then be willing to listen to what they tell you without proving them right!

Next time you feel anger rising, try to take a moment to imagine yourself in the other person's position before you lose control. Do you remember the characters in Charles Kingsley's children's book, *The Water Babies*? There was a *Mrs-Do-As-You-Would-Be-Done-By*, whose behavior was, as her name suggests, exemplary; and her opposite, *Mrs-Done-By-As-You-Did*, a far more alarming character, who catered to the

O beautiful one, one should forgive under every injury. It has been said that the continuation of species is due to man being forgiving. He, indeed, is a wise and excellent person who has conquered his wrath and shows forgiveness even when insulted, oppressed, and angered by a strong person. The man of power who controls his wrath, has (for his enjoyment) numerous everlasting regions; while he that is angry, is called foolish, and meets with destruction both in this and the other world.

KING YUDHISHTHIRA SPEAKING TO DRAUPADI IN THE MAHABHARATA:
VANA PARVA; SECTION XXVIII

willfully misbehaved. Which character's attention do you think your behavior would attract?

This is an old trick, but a good one: When you feel the red mist rising, count to three (or four, five, or ten if you can contain your rage that long) before you vent your anger. In that time do a quick re-evaluation of the situation. What are you really mad at: this person, what this person represents, or what he or she seems to imply—perhaps an apparent neglect or disrespect of you? Who does this person remind you of? Acknowledge the feeling but hold back your usual reaction. Don't indulge it. Change channels and think of something else. Later, when you've had a chance to cool off, take a quick mental review. See if you can guess where this particular trigger got started. You need to investigate this aspect of your past for its forgiveness potential if you want to stop knee-jerk reactions in the future.

Be ready with a deflecting ploy, such as, "I must be going now, there is something I have to attend to... " or some similar remark. Rather than giving in to your emotions, attempt to defuse potential explosions while you learn control. Pat yourself on the back whenever you manage to

66 *If a wicked man abandons his wickedness and repents, do not despise him.* 99

MIDRASH PROVERBS

walk away from an argument or strong reaction. Give yourself a reward of some sort. While mastering this skill, if you do boil over, don't berate yourself. No one is perfect and you tried your best. You can try again next time.

If your anger tends to be volcanic, holding back or deflecting will take a little practice. Telling yourself not to feel anger will seem like telling water to flow uphill. Begin by modifying your response to remind yourself that you are in control. Try not to be aggressive or abusive in your anger. Start with a little introspection when your temper flares; eventually you will get better at nipping it in the bud and assessing whether it is misplaced. Choose a word for silently centering yourself. When you feel the urge to rage, repeat this mantra to yourself. It can be as silly or relevant as you choose, but focusing on a specific word may help you ride out the inner storm. So what if someone catches you muttering "banana, banana, banana" to yourself; it may even make you smile!

Another enlightening exercise is to list the slights and old hostilities that you carry. Do you see a pattern? Do you recognize the attitudes of those who reared or taught you? Are these attitudes truly yours? Think about them. Is communication part of the problem? Could you empathize with the other person's position if the tables were turned? Does the perpetrator have any values or qualities that you appreciate, or do you see this person as unredeemably bad? Do you feel vulnerable in admitting your enemy has some good qualities because it lessens the hostility that has warmed you? Is it more important to you to win than to be freed? Why is this? When or where did you acquire this belief? Has it really served you well?

> 66 *Discretion is being able to raise your eyebrow instead of your voice.* 99

ANONYMOUS

66 *Write the bad things that are done to you in sand, but write the good things that happen to you on a piece of marble.* 99

ARABIC PARABLE

As you learn control, you may also notice patterns in what triggers your anger. Is there a common emotion, perhaps feeling bullied or ignored? Maybe during that "one–two–three," you will even be able to say, "There I go again. That was ____ speaking in me. I don't really think that way. Anyone can see this person is just ____. Why waste my anger on that?" With time, patience, humor, and practice you will assume more control of how and when and whether you lose your temper. Few people get it right every time, but each time you control your emotions you will feel stronger.

If you find certain activities or certain people always set you off, avoid them. Sit somewhere else, get on another bus, switch classes, change jobs. Do not expect more from yourself than you can manage.

Remember, perfection is not required. Just allow for what you recognize as thin ice. Your relationships will improve as you emanate less hostile energy, and you will attract kinder people.

It is possible to take a "holiday" from the pain you carry if the prospect of dropping it altogether is too daunting. (Letting go of the familiar can be alarming, even when the familiar is negative.) You may begin to see how much more effective you can be without your anger and pain than with them. You will certainly boost your physical and mental health. You will become a more effective caregiver, neighbor, coworker, friend, and family member when you put aside the exhaustion of grief or guilt or rage.

Set aside a time or activity during which you choose not to dwell on the pain. You can come back to it later, if you wish to—don't worry about that. Until you finish your chosen activity, convince yourself to put aside any and all thoughts on the subject that upset you. After this break, you may resume your feelings where you left off. It may seem hard to do this the first time, but persevere. The will to heal—which is within you—will welcome this opportunity to release your pain, so

> 66 *A wise man is superior to any insults which can be put upon him, and the best reply to unseemly behavior is patience and moderation.* 99

MOLIÈRE

relax. As you manage to put aside negative thoughts for longer and longer periods, you will discover something very important. Your suffering is a choice and a habit. It is not external. You can regain control. No one has been betrayed by your taking time out. No one has been let off the hook either—no one except you, that is.

Make an investment in a happier present by releasing the past. You change a position of weakness into one of power through the act of genuine forgiveness. What you do with today is what really matters. Make every day a chance to feel proud of yourself, even if only in small acts of generosity. Allow someone to go ahead of you in the supermarket line, especially if that person is frail, elderly, or has only a few items. Do you recall the "Practice random acts of kindness and senseless beauty" movement in the United States? Many people passing through toll booths on highways paid their own toll plus that for the car behind them, even though they didn't know the other driver. This generous anarchy spread into a popular movement. The givers enjoyed how their small acts of generosity made them feel, and those behind them reaped unexpected gifts. The habit spread to include theater and movie tickets and created happiness for as long as the craze lasted. How much more worthwhile this is than taking every petty opportunity to defraud, which leaves the cheater more diminished than the cheated. Look for the ways to be nicer to others; the reward that will flow back to you in good feeling will far outweigh your minimal effort. And you will surround yourself with positive energy instead of living as a sullen or angry person.

> 66 *Reject your sense of injury and the injury itself disappears.* 99
>
> MARCUS AURELIUS

Living Now, Not Then

❝The sun, though it passes through dirty places, yet remains as pure as before.❞

FRANCIS BACON

The first step in offering or accepting forgiveness is to honestly appraise what has happened. Until you have openly acknowledged the wrong, you cannot begin to forgive or free yourself from the pain you associate with the memory. You cannot change the past, but you can change your emotional response to it. Realize that it takes more energy to deny, block, or avoid facing the truth—and even more to hold on to anger or the desire for revenge—than it does to face the truth and deal with it openly. When you waste all this energy, you cannot

I was angry with my friend:
I told my wrath, my wrath did end.
I was angry with my foe:
I told it not, my wrath did grow.

WILLIAM BLAKE

use it to make the most of your present and future, to enjoy what life has yet to offer you.

The event that caused your pain is over even though its consequences may remain with you for the rest of your life. The sooner you release your attachment to your negative memories, the sooner you can recover and rebuild your life. You are much greater than your pain. If the past is so painful that you have blocked what happened, you have also cut yourself off from your real nature and depleted your energy. This can lead to self-alienation and the loss of purpose. But when you learn about yourself through negative events, you grow beyond them.

Refuse to allow your pain to continue to possess you. The focused obsession of love and hate are similar; you can fall out of hate just as you can fall out of love. Surrendering your anger may be the hardest thing in the world to contemplate, but it will be the easiest one to live with once you have.

Many religions, Buddhism primary among them, remind us to live in the present moment, for that is all we truly have. If we all stopped to think about this for a minute, we would know the truth of this statement and live accordingly, with profound effects. This is not to say that we should forgo goals and aspirations. Living in the present involves making the most of this moment while holding on to our dreams for tomorrow. Hope for the future, but live in the present. As the old saying goes, "Never put off until tomorrow what you can do today."

Why hold on to a bitterness from the past? As the Buddha reminded us, everything in the universe is changing at every moment, including ourselves, and we create our own suffering when we deny this and try to prevent change. We cannot invent a universe different from the one we occupy just because we do not like the rules that govern this one.

Most of us have a tendency to relive the past in our imagination, whether we found it good or ill, and each time we create a slightly different truth as memories fade. We base our expectations of the future on these reinvented truths, and daydream of a future that will never be; we can never include all the unforeseen influences that will subtly, or not so subtly, alter our best-laid plans. We all have biased or incomplete memories, even of events that we have witnessed. If you think about this for a moment or two, you will know it to be true. Sometimes you can know when you are deliberately altering a memory. It has been humorously suggested that we remember the future and imagine the past, when all we truly have is now.

> The past is dead, forget it,
> The future does not exist, don't worry,
> Today is here, use it.
>
> ANONYMOUS

Be Easy with Yourself

66 To be angry with the right person to the right extent and at the right time and with the right object and in the right way—that is not easy. 99

ARISTOTLE

*I*f you can, seek forgiveness for your own misguided acts and find a way to forgive others for theirs. You create your own torture as long as you hold on to the pain or need for restitution and retribution. Maybe you need to forgive yourself for something that only you know about. By nurturing feelings of guilt, shame, or anger, you burden yourself to no one's benefit. Make restitution if you can, and be as compassionate with yourself as you would be with another. In all likelihood, no one will view your actions as harshly as you do, not even the person you feel you wronged. Most of us set higher standards for ourselves than we would for anyone else. How would you counsel a friend who regretted a similar action? Why treat yourself any more harshly than you would your friend? We are all part of the Divine, all chips off the same block. Can you imagine Jesus, Muhammad, the Buddha, or any other realized soul berating you or failing to extend compassion toward you? Why place yourself above such beings in deciding you deserve a harsher judgment?

If you caused hurt to another for which you seek forgiveness, take steps to avoid acting in the same way again, whatever the provocation. Learn to control yourself. Accepting forgiveness without an intent to change is just hollow rhetoric. Commit yourself through action, not just words or good intentions. Find a counselor to help you if it is within your means and you think you will benefit. Change may not come easily or immediately, but forgiveness is worthwhile, and so are you.

Can you ask the person you wronged to forgive you? Carefully consider the possible implications of your desire for absolution. If you must confess something that would cause another's pain, take it to the professionals instead; find a counselor or priest who will listen in strict confidence and help release you from your burden of guilt. If you cannot bear to tell anyone, give your pain to God. His shoulders are broad enough to bear it, and He will absolve you. Perhaps you have to forgive yourself in secret, or you have no faith in a God. If so, make a small ritual to rid yourself of past feelings. Imbue some object with your sorrow and guilt, then bury it, burn it, or otherwise destroy it—with its destruction feel yourself become free from torment.

If it is too soon to think of forgiveness for yourself or for another, give yourself the time you need. Until you can accept the truth of what happened and why, you cannot begin to forgive and move on with your life. But only you can decide when the time feels right.

66 *Remember, people will judge you by your actions, not your intentions. You may have a heart of gold—but so does a hard-boiled egg.* 99

ANONYMOUS

You Have Choices

❝ True forgiveness is a willingness to change your mind about your Self. ❞

ROBERT HOLDEN

With forgiveness come choice and responsibility. You must decide if you can accept or bestow forgiveness, and you control when and whether it is more appropriate to express blame than to express forgiveness. Each choice that you make has consequences. If you choose to withhold forgiveness, you must find a positive way to contain your pain or risk allowing it to affect your health and relationships. Whatever you decide, find a way to release the energy spent on restraining your anger.

Not all anger is bad; it can be an essential survival tool. Remaining placid in the face of danger is unrealistic and foolhardy. The spiritually developed person knows and accepts his or her true self, including the rise of anger when the occasion demands it. Jesus did not petition the money lenders to leave the temple—He threw them out. But learn how to use your anger with discrimination. Enough and no more. If you experience real and immediate physical threat, for example, or if you witness cruelty toward another—human or animal—and you can safely make a difference, be enlivened by your anger. Use it in the service of a political cause; to empower a creative endeavor; to rescue a person in mortal danger; when you need to run the fastest mile. Do you recall the woman who lifted a car to rescue a child trapped beneath it? When asked by journalists to repeat the feat when not fired by urgent need, she could not lift the car again. Artists who rely on their anguish for inspiration may choose to keep their pain rather than risk losing their creativity. Some of the most creative artists and original thinkers have allegedly been hard to live with. It seems that their creativity came at the expense of social niceties.

66 To be wronged is nothing unless you continue to remember it. **99**

CONFUCIUS

57

Once you know your pain and how to contain it appropriately, you have access to a major energy conduit, instead of a messy, spluttering rage. Use it as your powerhouse, as long as the effort of keeping a lid on your anger until you need it does not consume you, and as long as it does not affect the innocent.

However, bottling up anger may not always enhance creativity. It can, instead, deaden all responses to life and in giving or receiving forgiveness you might find that a tidal wave of blocked creativity is released. Always seek out ways to express your anger that will not harm others, even those who you believe deserve your vengeance. Try to use your feelings creatively rather than negatively if at all possible. You might find you can channel your feelings of energy through art, writing, or sports or other types of physical activity. Perhaps you could spring clean the house or dig the garden. Use this channeling activity to metaphorically count to three. Permit your honest feelings to well up so that you can live through them, but do so in a contained environment that will not extend your problems.

Evaluate the Misdeeds

66 *Father, forgive them for they know not what they do.* 99

AMONG THE LAST WORDS OF JESUS,
SPOKEN FROM HIS AGONY ON THE CROSS; LUKE 23:34

orgiveness is an ongoing practice, not a single act. It cannot be accomplished in an afternoon, unless the offence is very minor and recent. Here we will assume the wounds are older and greater, as these are the hardest to forgive. If we have allowed a wound to fester, it spreads into other areas of our life and becomes harder to heal. Even more difficult are those wrongs that were endured repeatedly, until our reactions became dulled and our appropriate anger buried deep. Such hurts do not go away after a moment's well-intended or insincere absolution. Forgiveness requires a generous and sincere change of heart following a profound attitude and belief alteration. This demands constant work.

When we truly forgive, we reach an understanding that allows us to forgo anger or grief. We become ready to let go of the past, despite its painful memories—but not the memories themselves. These remain though we do not dwell on them. The emotional undertow lessens and is brought under control; most of the time, at any rate. We accept, however reluctantly, that we cannot change the past, and become willing to move forward. Through forgiveness of the wrongdoer, and ourselves, we can learn to love and laugh again. We choose to embrace the present, to move on to whatever new experiences life has in store for us, and to face them strengthened by our survival.

How is it possible to forgive what we cannot forget? It is difficult to move past the anger and hurt that fate, neglect, or malicious acts have bestowed, and no one should pretend otherwise. Pride may also be at stake, especially if we have taken a public stance against the wrongdoers. If we have wounded others and wish to find forgiveness, we may live with guilt and shame. In either case, the past and its emotional fallout can affect the quality of our life. Forgiveness offers us a return to sanity, if we are able to use it.

You may ask why the one who caused pain should be released from responsibility or accountability. We all nurse the wish that life were fair. And holding on to anger offers us the impression of control in an otherwise powerless situation. The grudge may have even created a sense of moral superiority, but while you spent energy on remaining enraged, hating the perpetrator, you suffered the most. The object of your resentment was not hurt in the least. In fact the contrary could be the case. If someone hurt you deliberately, your continued anguish could increase his or her satisfaction. You, however, need to be released from the grip of bitterness. All the while you nursed your grievance, however justified, you imprisoned yourself through your inability to let go of the pain. However unjustly, your continuing feelings of hurt and anger cause the historical event to continue to persecute and upset you. You are the one keeping the pain alive. How long will you continue to do this?

66 Forgiveness is the answer to the child's dream of a miracle by which what is broken is made whole again, what is soiled is made clean again. 99

DAG HAMMARSKJÖLD

How and whether you free yourself will depend on your circumstances, how great the cause for hurt, whether you can surmount your pain or loss, and whether you can find the ability to forgive. If you can, you will reclaim control and release yourself from bondage. The forgiver gains more than the forgiven, without a doubt, but as with all acts of charity, the motivation should be selfless if it is to be genuine. This is easier said than done, as we shall see.

Regrettably some people suffered so much as children that they learned to shut down their feelings in order to survive with some semblance of sanity. To be powerless against regular abuse or violence in full awareness doubles the pain. In this position, many learn to split off their feelings from events. Such individuals may subsequently find it hard to understand when, as adults, their actions cause pain to others. Because their own feeling nature has closed down, perhaps irretrievably, they no longer have access to empathy or sympathy. To judge such a person as you would yourself is inappropriate. Rather than hate them for their actions, sympathy might be more appropriate. They have no training in society's ground rules, and we should not be

❝To forgive is the highest, most beautiful form of love.

In return, you will receive untold peace and happiness.❞

ROBERT MULLER

surprised if they have acquired different, perhaps horrifying, life strategies. Past maladjustment may be redeemed, but usually only after the offenders have been burned by others' reactions to their antisocial behavior. If a habitual response ceases to work well, they may decide to reform, but if the fear of losing the protective wall of unfeeling is too great, they may never change. Consider the barriers you have to granting forgiveness and whether they are justified here.

We all make mistakes, but absolution is for God alone to grant because only He knows the wider implications of any act. When we forgive, we do so as God's agent, since what we bestow is not really within our gifts. In the process we free ourselves from negative attachments to past events, but we grant forgiveness only after judging the circumstances, perhaps after an apology, and only if the personal cost is not too great and the rewards worthwhile. We determine the conditions under which we are willing to forgive, yet we never possess all the facts when we make our judgment. This is why it is said:

> **“To err is human, to forgive, divine.”**
>
> ALEXANDER POPE

66 *He who angers you*

In forgiving we do not condone the act. Wrongdoing is the responsibility of the wrongdoer, an act of ego, and appropriate punishment may be meted out according to the law. Forgiveness, however, is for the heart, not the law. Whatever the transgression, forgiveness is given from soul to soul. God's forgiveness requires no preconditions and demands no prior apologies. It is given to us unconditionally.

But what if you feel you need to forgive God? Some experiences can shake our faith—to the point of expressing anger at our core beliefs. How can an all-knowing God allow bad things to happen to good people? How can he allow them to die, be maimed, or become critically *conquers you.*"

ELIZABETH KENNY

ill? Or do you need to forgive the person whose death deprived you of his or her companionship, support, and security? To rail against God or the dead may seem shameful, but it is far from unusual. In the expression of honest anguish, it is a healthy and reasonable reaction. Don't worry. God can take it, and as for our dead loved ones if we knew them well enough to feel it they knew us well enough to understand our anger.

The more often we fail to be honest about how we feel, whatever the consequences, the more we become like Gulliver captured by the Lilliputians, tied by a million little restraints. With each self-denial we move farther and farther from our true being and potential. If you find it really difficult to let the anger go, perhaps it has become how you define yourself; would it threaten your very

66 *Do to others what you would have them do to you.* **99**

BIBLE

identity to put it aside? Start by pretending. As we do, so we become. Fake it until it becomes a habit and then a genuine response. (Most learning happens that way.) You had to learn to ride a bicycle, and even to walk, by feigning confidence and suffering a few spills in your early attempts. Have sincere intention and be prepared for a few accidents, but make a start. The longest part of the journey is that first step.

Forgiving others permits us to erase past judgments and brings a sense of relief. I should confess here that I must regularly tackle my reluctance to forgive: over the books I have loaned that were not returned; over the disappointment of being deceived by one I thought I could trust; over my parents being less skilled at their roles than I could have wished. Everyone has such a list. I won't change the past by my forgiving; the books are still missing, the deceit did happen, my parents are no longer alive so they will not change. What is different is the energy I no longer waste, pointlessly wishing the past were different. Stuff happens. Let the past be the past and make room for the present.

Intent

66 *Resentment is a poison one takes, hoping to harm another.* 99

ANONYMOUS

*B*efore judging another's actions we should understand the intent behind them. We would hesitate to judge if the culprit were an animal, a child, a person suffering from dementia or other illness, someone unaware of the consequences of his or her actions. Perhaps the event was an accident. We may have regret, but surely there is nothing to condemn? Once we start to consider these exceptions we may wonder whether most, if not all, wrongdoers have mitigating circumstances that surround their actions. What might we have done if we were in their shoes? Would the misdeed become more understandable? Was it prompted by the need for survival rather than wickedness? Could you really hold a lifelong grudge against such an action? Have you never acted irresponsibly? Did you never lie to or cheat your parents, ever? Did you get away with it, or were you found out, but forgiven? None of us are immune from foolish actions. Unfortunately sometimes they get out of hand. Do you want to tie yourself for life to someone else's lack of judgment?

Forgiveness has to be heartfelt and constantly renewed; it is not a barter for something you want. You cannot swap forgiveness for better health, sleep, or peace of mind. Nevertheless, you will receive these things with forgiveness. The process, not the show of forgiveness, can truly transform. Anger and resentment, which tend to follow the inability to forgive, can lead to physical, emotional, or mental problems—insomnia, anxiety, hypertension, heart troubles, strokes, lowered immunity, headaches, loss of appetite or compensatory overeating and obesity-related illnesses, even cancers. Your emotional fragility, depression, or anger may also adversely affect your friends, family, and coworkers. The pressure of denying yourself, avoiding exposure, or not trusting others more likely results from an awareness of your own lapses. In any case, taking a risk and forgiving has to be less damaging than holding on to pain or guilt. It is a fair bet that the person who wronged you will not have suffered for as long as you have. Those events took place once, perhaps long ago. Your scenario has been taking place daily ever since.

You suffer no loss when you freely give, no sorrow where there is no loss. Anger becomes pointless, and peace and serenity will eventually return. Forgive or seek forgiveness if you can.

❝ I learned that it is the weak who are cruel, and that gentleness is to be expected only from the strong. ❞

LEO ROSTEN

> 66 *If you are patient in one moment of anger, you will escape a hundred days of sorrow.* 99

CHINESE PROVERB

■ Forgiveness

Resentment and Anger —Who Suffers?

« He who seeks revenge should dig two graves. »

CHINESE PROVERB

How good are you at forgiving when someone apologizes? Would you rather keep your anger and resentment? If you can find it in your heart to forgive, you can end an intolerable situation in which you suffer as much, if not more, than the subject of your anger. You can move into a brighter future. If you cannot forgive, you have chosen to nurse your anger and keep the pain alive. Your own regret and disappointment ensnares you in an imaginary land of what might have been and keeps you from the potential for happiness. Maybe you feel another has spoiled the best part of you. Realize there is so much more to who you are, what you can do, and where you can find joy. Do not tie yourself to the one negative person or thing. You can choose to perpetuate the misery, or move away from it and allow the past to rest in peace.

Forgiveness is not easy to give or to receive. If others do harm to us, they remain accountable for their actions whether or not we forgive them. Our forgiveness cannot alter facts. One of the hardest hurts to forgive is the loss of a loved one through another's carelessness or deliberate act. We blame ourselves, other people, even God.

The Buddha is said to have comforted a grieving widow who asked him to bring her husband back to life. He used a kindly ploy that enabled her to accept death as a natural part of life. He did not agree to or deny her request but instead asked her to bring him a mustard seed (common in Indian kitchens) from a house where no death had occurred. Thinking he needed this for a magic ritual, perhaps, the widow set off. After a long and fruitless search she realized that no such

> ***If we could read the secret history of our enemies, we should find in each person's life sorrow and suffering enough to disarm all hostility.*** **
>
> HENRY WADSWORTH LONGFELLOW

house existed, and she returned to the Buddha, finally able to accept her own loss. She so appreciated the gentle way the Buddha had re-educated her that she became one of the first Buddhist nuns.

The widow had realized, with the Buddha's help, that she was the agent of her own suffering. Her husband's death was a natural event, not an extraordinary one. Once she realized that death touches every family, she accepted the inevitability of death and was released from her pain.

A quotation from the Hindu collected tales called *The Bhagavad Gita* reminds us not to fear death; it is a temporary transition in the life of a soul that never dies.

The wise do not grieve for the dead or the living. Never was there a time when I was not, nor you, nor these others, nor will there ever be a time when we shall cease to be. As the soul passes in this body through childhood, youth and old age, even so it is taking on another body. The sage is not perplexed by this.

THE BHAGAVAD GITA

When anger or resentment eats at our soul, it is not just us who suffer the consequences. Our emotions and subsequent actions will certainly affect the lives of everyone around us—from friends to family—and, in particular, those younger than ourselves. The quality of care that we give our children is very important. What we pass on to them can reflect our growth as individuals, despite the trials that we have endured, or it can doom them to the same influences that have damaged us. Whether we mean to or not, we can negatively affect the next generation, who look to us for guidance, if we do not seek help to sort these issues out. In order to celebrate and affirm the experiences of a new beginning, we must learn to let go of the anger that we sometimes feel. Let the suffering end with you. When we forgive, we offer our young charges a positive model for avoiding resentment and for handling painful situations constructively.

“Resentments are burdens we don't need to carry.**”**

ANONYMOUS

Stuff Happens —
How Do You React?

*66 How much more grievous are the consequences
of anger than the causes of it.99*

MARCUS AURELIUS

*T*ry answering the following questions. They may reveal to you how your personal expectations dictate your ability to forgive, be forgiven, and experience joy. There are no "right" answers. It may help to write your feelings on a piece of paper so that you can clearly and objectively think about your true emotions.

- Are you afraid to forgive?

- Would you feel disloyal to yourself or another if, by forgiving a wrongdoer, you were freed from bitterness?

- Have you been hurt and angry so often that you feel most comfortable with those emotions? Are you a little suspicious or afraid of happiness?

- If a good experience happens to you, do you automatically look for reasons why it will not last, cannot be as good as it seems, or is bound to end badly?

- Are you less comfortable with praise than with criticism?

- Do you deserve to be happy?

- Do you fear that others will dislike you if you enjoy good fortune and believe friendship depends on sharing your miseries?

- Is happiness only to be expected in another life, never in this one?

- Is suffering a necessary part of life?

- Do you expect to be happy in the future? If so, what will have changed between now and then?

- Is happiness impossible?

- If you decided not to grant forgiveness to someone, could anyone else do it on your behalf? Would this help you?
- Who would be pleased to see you happy?
- Who would be irritated by your happiness, and why?
- Can material acquisitions compensate for unhappiness?
- What do you feel when you buy stuff or overeat? Are you responding to a lack, or do these actions blunt or mask an older craving?
- In childhood did you feel loved and appreciated for yourself, despite any faults or misdeeds?

Our reactions to life events can reveal a lot about us. They can teach us why we are in pain and how we might seek or offer forgiveness.

66*Yet Man is born into trouble, as the sparks fly upward.*99

JOB 5:7 KJV

Forgiveness Is a State of Mind

Forgiveness means letting go of the past.

GERALD JAMPOLSKY

*P*erhaps your pain stems from a long-term relationship rather than a traumatic single event. If you need a place to start investigating its source, the family can often prove fruitful ground. Take a look at the family photo album for triggers to past memories. What do you see in the pictures? Does the posture or body language of anyone portrayed reveal something? Look at how relatives are positioned. Does anyone often stand or sit apart, an outsider in the group? Take note of the absences too. Who's missing?

Do you look happy? Do you remember actually feeling happy? Are there photographs from your childhood? If no, why not? Be prepared to revisit the pain of childhood disappointments in this exercise. If your family was the seat of your trauma, your responses may shock and upset you. Use what you learn to see whether forgiveness would heal your relations with these people, or whether it would help you. Ask your brothers and sisters about their childhood memories. How do they explain the things you see in the photographs? Siblings can have very different parenting experiences.

66 *Even an enemy must be offered appropriate hospitality, if he comes to your home. A tree does not deny its shade to the one who comes to cut it down.* 99

MAHABHARATA, XII, 374

" If there is something to pardon in everything, there is also something to condemn. "

FRIEDRICH NIETZSCHE

The unforgiving mind is full of fear, and offers love no room to be itself; no place where it can spread its wings in peace and soar above the turmoil of the world. The unforgiving mind is sad, without the hope of respite and release from pain. It suffers and abides in misery, peering about in darkness, seeing not, yet certain of the danger lurking there.

The unforgiving mind is torn with doubt, confused about itself and all it sees; afraid and angry, weak and blustering, afraid to go ahead, afraid to stay, afraid to waken or to go to sleep, afraid of every sound, yet more afraid of stillness; terrified of darkness, yet more terrified at the approach of light.

A COURSE IN MIRACLES, FOUNDATION FOR INNER PEACE

If you can now see that these people are flawed humans rather than intentionally vindictive, forgiveness becomes easier. As you lay their demons to rest, you may unearth your own; but in bringing them to the surface, you may be able to forgive yourself too. You were just doing your best with the limited skills of a child. These are the people who should have known better. If they did not, why not? Do they deserve your pity? Do you have compassion for the child you were?

This exercise can provide a useful doorway to forgiveness, but only attempt it in a controlled and safe atmosphere. If you are lonely or vulnerable or have no one to comfort you, this might prove too risky a venture. Listen to your inner voice. If your family is accessible, and you can now show your relatives compassion and, most important, feel compassion toward them, you will also reap the benefit. As the desire for retaliation recedes, you will experience ever greater feelings of compassion and generosity. Even if family members have died, you can still start to heal old wounds by learning about them as people, instead of relying on them to fill the roles that were relevant to your childhood. As an adult you can fend for yourself and you can also seek out professional and personal help.

Accept Your Feelings

66 *Innumerable people are angry without any reason; a large number are angry for a reason; there are only a few who are not getting angry even if they have a reason.* **99**

SUBHASHITARNAVA, 83

When you are able to acknowledge and accept your true feelings, only then you will be ready to find alternatives to the responses that you've developed over the years. Jack Kornfield, in his book *A Path With a Heart*, beautifully describes the Buddhist approach of opening ourselves to an awareness of feelings:

In a teaching called the Arising of Conditions, the Buddha explains how humans become entangled. It is the place of feeling that binds us or frees us. When pleasant feelings arise and we automatically grasp them, or when unpleasant feelings arise and we try to avoid them, we set up a chain reaction of entanglement and suffering. This perpetuates the body of fear. However if we learn to be aware of feelings without grasping or aversion, then they can move through us like changing weather, and we can be free to feel them and move on like the wind.

As the Buddha reminds us, it is our attachment to our feelings that causes suffering. We become attached to pleasurable things because we don't wish to lose them and attached to nonpleasurable things because they arouse strong emotions.

66 *Anger and jealousy can no more bear to lose sight of their objects than love.* **99**

GEORGE ELIOT

If you honestly examine your anger or desire for revenge, you may discover that they mask deeper feelings, such as:

- shame or guilt (and anger toward the situation or person who precipitated these feelings)
- betrayal (and anger at the dishonor or lack of respect shown to you)
- grief (and anger for a loss you could not prevent, but would have wished to, or for being deserted—a reminder that you are not always in control)
- helplessness (and anger at realizing that control is always illusory)

If you have ever given in to your anger and sought revenge, were you really seeking to restore your sense of power (and with it the comfortable illusion of "being in control")? Apart from the futility of such a mission, when you give in to thoughts of revenge, you actually expand the original hurt. Your rage keeps your pain and its cause ever present in your life. You have made the choice to eat, sleep, and walk with your target by activating your hatred. There is as much intimacy in hatred as in loving desire. In both cases our focus seldom wavers. Many believe it is easier to lash out than to revise their beliefs and face the risk of appearing weak or foolish, or worse, by forgiving.

Forgiving involves a degree of compassion and understanding that might rob you of your moral indignation and the right to rage. When you feel helpless and out of control, these are welcome substitutes. Understanding and compassion, on the other hand, seem to ask even more of you, when you may feel you have already given too much. But, remember, *compassion and forgiveness always benefit the giver more than the one given to*. You carried the pain and you can release it. Think about that. The focus of your anger has never been touched by your feelings, and while your forgiveness may be welcome and may alleviate any guilt or sorrow, the one you forgave has never carried the burden of corrosive hatred you have. If you forgive, you do not deny what you feel or what happened, and you may never forget. You do not absolve wrongdoers from responsibility for their actions either. If you cannot yet forgive, have compassion for yourself and the suffering you must continue to experience. You feelings are valid, and your decision is right for you.

Reframe the Issue:

You Are Not Your Pain

66 These are man's intercessors: repentance and good deeds. 99

TALMUD

*I*f you still need vengeance, consider for a moment why and what good it would serve. Be sure of your motive. Does raging at others mask responsibility a little nearer to home? Would it in any way alter the past? Would the proof that you can act as irresponsibility as the one who hurt you advance your case against that person? Would you be open to a more constructive approach? Reframe the way you view the situation; give it a different slant. Here are some suggestions to get you started.

Consider how the perpetrator may be feeling. If you have ever wronged someone, did you feel worse than you do now? Is it perhaps more difficult to bear guilt than blame? Do you always have to win? Can you accept that, at times, conceding defeat is the only victory available? Do you hold the belief that only the weak forgive while those with any guts retaliate? Where did you first learn that? Is it easier to blame than to forgo retaliation and forgive? After all, many people would understand your motives for revenge while your compassion might take more explaining. Have you ever needed to be forgiven? How good are you at accepting blame when you have made a mistake? Is there always a "but ... " in your case, while others are clearly at fault? Do you dwell on the person you blame? Try changing your focus whenever the painful incident enters your mind by concentrating on another topic. Do you tend toward passive aggression, muttering, gossiping, finding fault? Have you ever tried to see the good in people first? Try being a little more positive towards your friends, family, and work colleagues for one whole day and see how it feels. Resist the urge to retaliate when you feel provoked, and make only affirmative and positive responses. After such a day, reflect. Did people react differently to you? How did it make you feel? If you can choose which channels to play in your head, why have you chosen to replay the painful one?

> Forgiveness paints a picture of a world where suffering is over, loss becomes impossible and anger makes no sense. Attack is gone, and madness has an end. What suffering is now conceivable? What loss can be sustained? The world becomes a place of joy, abundance, charity and endless giving.
>
> A COURSE IN MIRACLES: WORKBOOK FOR STUDENTS, LESSON 249,
> "FORGIVENESS ENDS ALL SUFFERING AND LOSS"

66 In essence, true forgiveness is the willingness to believe

(1) you are whole;

(2) no one can threaten or take away your wholeness. 99

ROBERT HOLDEN

Wholeness
Cannot Be Diminished

" Be kind and compassionate to one another, forgiving each other, just as in Christ God forgave you."

EPHESIANS 4:32

When you can forgive, you can also embrace the love and wholeness that was always there. You become willing to risk trust and hope rather than fear and despair. In the process, you will lift the pain you have carried. Know that you are as worthy and deserving of love and happiness as any other being. You are so much more than your fears, mistakes, or self-doubt. You can be complete without receiving repayment for the debt created in your life. Bad things happen to us all at times.

We are constantly surrounded by and immersed in love, though we may choose to believe otherwise. If we have turned our faces away, we can choose to turn back to the light within us at any time. The light was never diminished.

" Forgive your enemies, but never forget their names. "

JOHN FITZGERALD KENNEDY

❝ The Soul is without beginning and without end. Immersed in one's Soul one should move and act without giving way to wrath, without giving in to joy, and always free from envy. Cutting the knots in one's heart one should live happily without giving way to grief and with one's doubts dispelled.❞

MAHABHARATA XII, 149

Forgiveness —
To Conceal or Reveal?

❝ *You attract what you believe you deserve.* ❞

ROBERT HOLDEN

orgiving does not mean forgetting. You may never forget the past, nor wish to, but you cannot begin to forgive until you have faced and accepted the facts. As long as you bury your feelings and refuse to examine events in your past, you will remain locked in a dark room. Perhaps you have found it hard to forgive because you hold mixed feelings toward the agent of your unhappiness. Only you can know if exposing the truth will cause more pain than good. Only you can decide whether forgiveness is possible.

How then to proceed if your need to forgive is entwined with your need for connection and attention? Do you reveal all in order to heal your wounds and move on to forgiveness? Or do you continue to conceal the truth and allow the wounds to fester because of the possible consequences? Many feel the need to protect those to whom their anger or forgiveness might rightly be directed. Especially so if the wrongdoer is a parent, in a position of authority, or publicly renowned. You may fear exposure and ridicule for being thought malicious. Why should anyone listen to you—especially if you were a child when the event took place? Maybe in telling the truth you would suffer a further loss. An abusive parent, for example, will probably evoke mixed feelings of anger and need in a victim, even years later. The role of parent is important and formative for each of us. We continue to expect the

❝ *They who forgive most shall be most forgiven.* ❞

JOSIAH BAILEY

109

> *66 The ineffable joy of forgiving and being forgiven forms an ecstasy that might well arouse the envy of the gods. 99*
>
> ELBERT HUBBARD

model parent, even though the imperfect or abusive person who actually filled that role repeatedly showed us that our expectations were unreasonable. We still fear the loss of that perfect parent, regardless of the behavior of the one we had. Accepting inappropriate attention may seem preferable to risking life with *no* parental attention. We all need to belong, and our parents, of whatever caliber, seem vital. The need for a parent can continue to outweigh the need to expose the actions of the person who bears the title, and you should not feel pressured to alter the dynamic unless you are ready and well supported. This sort of dilemma really does need professional help to disentangle. What is impossibly difficult for us to make sense of is daily fare for them. There are also many organizations that offer help to the powerless; if

" To carry a grudge is like being stung to death by one bee. "

WILLIAM H. WALTON

you would like to expose the truth, to forgive or otherwise, contact someone who can give you confidential moral and legal support.

Could you approach the person who hurt you to say now what you could not say before? This is not an exercise in domination or a chance to fight old battles. Can you express what you felt without aggression or hostility, as a simple sharing of fact? Could you listen to his or her point of view? Have you gained any insights since the original offence? Can you share these now? If the situation is irretrievable, can you let it and this person go, and release the burden of resentment you have carried?

You might prefer to "speak" to this person in a letter. Pour out your feelings and make your letter as long as you need. This format can alleviate the discomfort of a face-to-face confrontation. A letter can also allow you to express honest feelings to someone who has died, to God, to your guardian angel, to your cancer, to your body. You do not need to send your letter. In some cases, it might be wise not to; for example, to your parents, whose goodwill you still need despite your resentments, your boss, your teacher, your children. Work out what you feel—the anger, sadness, regret or bitterness, the fears and shame.

Even if the person has died or otherwise gone away, expressing how you feel is still important, valid, and possible through writing. If you do decide to send your letter, realize that the recipient may disagree with your version of what happened; your writings will inevitably spring from your experience of the event, not gold-plated truth. What is important is that you openly admit all the feelings you have nursed and suppressed. If the person has died, you may gain resolution by reading your letter aloud at the graveside. If the person has moved elsewhere and you contemplate sending the letter, be aware that it might be read by others and might cause pain to innocent parties. Also be mindful of whether your words could be considered libelous.

If you write purely to express your most honest feelings, you can let rip without fear; no one else will ever see it. You might create a ceremonial burial or burn your writing to symbolize your separation from the past and the beginning of a new future in which, though not forgotten, the person who hurt you will not dominate and dictate your life.

Some therapists recommend an extension to this exercise. After you have honestly expressed your side of the story, compose a second letter.

Fortitude, forgiveness, self-control, abstention from unlawful gain, purity of body and mind, sense control, study of scriptures, meditation on the Supreme, truthfulness, freedom from anger — this is the tenfold path of virtue.

MANUSMRITI, VI, 92

In this one, reply as the person to whom you have just written. What does that person say in his or her defense or by way of explanation for the situation? (You may know of reasons for granting compassion and forgiveness and be willing to "hear" them now that you have had your rant.) Write what you wish that person had said in real life. Would you have him or her apologize, explain, express love for you? When you are ready, write a third letter (as yourself this time), offering forgiveness, if you can do so sincerely. If that is still beyond your capability, write of how you hope to reach the stage where forgiveness will be possible. Continue to write such letters from time to time until the forgiveness comes naturally.

The fear of being disloyal can create a strong barrier to forgiveness. We may feel we owe it to a third party to not forgive the wrongdoer. We may even feel we must exact vengeance on another's behalf, particularly if the victim is unable to seek redress in person. This often occurs when we wish to protect and honor someone who has died. We can become trapped by this emotionally charged loyalty as any act of forgiveness could seem an act of betrayal.

You may forgive and still choose not to reconcile with those you have forgiven. Whether you wish them to be a part of your future life is an entirely separate decision. But do let them go from your emotional life; through forgiving them, and yourself, bury the ghosts of your past.

Occasionally, pain may be associated with events that happened before our birth. Some people are affected by the history of their family, race, faith, or country. Such collective negativity extends far beyond immediate or personal experience. Indeed where wrongdoing occurred to a whole race or religious group, it may seem disloyal to our very identity to consider forgiveness. But this misconstrues the meaning of forgiveness. In fact we only forgive where wrong has been committed and blame is deserved. Forgiveness follows evil or error, not accident or misfortune. If it were not so, we might settle for an excuse or an apology. We in no sense condone the wrongdoing and certainly will not accept such behavior in the future.

What we must do, however, is admit to ourselves just what happened, how we felt about it then and feel about it now, and be ready to forgive ourselves for having been powerless to change what happened. We need to hold on to what the experience has taught us, but do so freed from the pain with which we associate the memory. Only when we have forgiven ourselves can we really hope to forgive the other person or persons involved and be free of the burden we have carried. We cannot ever turn back the clock and have things be other than as they were. What we can do is free ourselves from the resentment, pain, or anger that we have bottled up ever since.

Give yourself the gift of forgiveness. Give up the vain hope that by holding on to the pain, you will somehow make the past better. This moment is all that you have. You cannot change past experiences. They were what they were; but they were then, not now. When you can let them go, and happiness returns, you will find yourself in a much more secure place. From this position of strength, you can be magnanimous with your forgiveness without great personal cost. All it takes is your choice to allow a different attitude. Happiness was always with you.

A wise man will make haste to forgive, because he knows the full value of time and will not suffer it to pass away in unnecessary pain.

SAMUEL JOHNSON

66 This my son
was dead and
is alive again;
he was lost
and is found. 99

LUKE 15:24

Self-Forgiveness

❝ To forgive is to set a prisoner free and discover that the prisoner was you. ❞

LEWIS SMEDES

Sad to say, but until you can forgive yourself, you are unlikely to be able to forgive anyone else. You may ask what forgiveness you could possibly need. Surely you have no reason to seek forgiveness from anyone when you were the victim of a situation, not its agent. Perhaps you feel partly responsible, or fear you might have done more to prevent what happened. How about the times when you have betrayed your higher aspirations and behaved badly, then criticized yourself because you did? Have you forgiven yourself for when you acted out of fear, were judgmental or unkind? Why do you imagine you acted that way? Have you forgiven yourself for so needing love that you went to extreme lengths to feel loved? Did you act in some way that encouraged a bad experience? Should you have said something sooner or taken a different route or listened to your intuition? Do you feel responsible, or partially responsible, for some other act, or failure to act? Are these such awful crimes?

When you feel anger and hatred for another, it is often a projection of the anger and hatred you have for yourself. You find the faults in others that you know you exhibit and become irritated by having them brought to your notice. When you have compassion for your own failings, you may find yourself more tolerant of the failings of others. So with forgiveness. You cannot forgive in another what you cannot forgive in yourself.

❝ *God will forgive me; it is His trade.* ❞

HEINRICH HEINE

> Laugh and the world laughs with you;
> Weep, and you weep alone;
> For the sad old earth must borrow its mirth,
> But has trouble enough of its own.
>
> ELLA WHEELER WILCOX

It can sometimes be easier to blame ourselves than those really responsible. It can also be easier to blame than to accept that random crimes and tragedies happen all the time. There need be no premotivation or justification or sense to what happened. Sometimes people are unlucky enough to be at the wrong place at the wrong time, by pure chance. Had it not been you or your loved one, it would have been someone else. Would that have been any more just? Get in the habit of forgiving yourself, and forgiving others will become easier.

Others take their cues from us. How you feel about yourself affects how you feel about others. If we feel and act ashamed, those around us will become uncomfortable, then our poor self-esteem will seem justified. While some have enormous hurdles to overcome, for most of us, if we can make light of our troubles, we will find willing helpers and a ready smile. If we can be forgiving of others, we are more likely to accept forgiveness when it is offered to us.

Life is 5 percent what happens to you and 95 percent what you make of what happens to you. You do have choices at all times. Yes, bad and sad things happen—to everyone—but whether you let them color your life or just add shade and contour to it is up to you. Holding on to

66 *Almost all our faults are more pardonable than the methods we think up to hide them.* 99

ANONYMOUS

anguish does nothing to alter material facts or bring back a time past. It does do a huge amount to ruin your present, and the present makes up your future. Forgiving is a decision you are free to make. Some make it early, some late, some not at all, but it is a gift available to each of us.

For a long time it had seemed to me that life was about to begin — real life. But there was always some obstacle in the way, something to be got through first, some unfinished business, time still to be served, a debt to be paid. Then life would begin. At last it dawned on me that these obstacles were my life.

FR. ALFRED D'SOUZA

66 *Those who have understood
the connection between all
things do not shed tears; for the
one who looks at everything
with right understanding there
are no tears.* 99

MAHABHARATA, **XII**, 317

Picture Credits

pages 2 and 54: Hans Memling (c.1433-94). Louvre/Bridgeman Art Library.

pages 10–11: George Pierre Seurat (1859–91). Courtauld Institute Gallery, Somerset House, London/Bridgeman Art Library.

page 17: Suzuki Harunobu (1725–70). Art Institute of Chicago/Bridgeman Art Library.

page 27: George Pierre Seurat (1859–91). Glasgow Art Gallery and Museum/Bridgeman Art Library.

pages 32–33: Katsushika Hokusai (1760–1849). Christie's Images/Bridgeman Art Library.

pages 44–45: Peder Severin Kroyer (1851–1909). Skagens Museum/Bridgeman Art Library.

pages 56–57: Chinese School (19th Century). Phillips, The International Fine Art Auctioneers/Bridgeman Art Library.

pages 70–71: Vincent van Gogh (1853–90). Folkwang Museum/Bridgeman Art Library.

page 76: Utagawa Kunisada (1786–1864). Maidstone Museum and Art Gallery/Bridgeman Art Library.

pages 82–83: Felix Edouard Vallotton (1865–1925). Musee d'Orsay/Peter Willi/Bridgeman Art Library.

pages 92–93: Caspar David Friedrich (1774–1840). Pushkin Museum/Bridgeman Art Library.

pages 96–97: by Gustave Courbet (1819–77). National Gallery of Scotland/Bridgeman Art Library.

page 106: Indian School (19th century). Royal Asiatic Society/Bridgeman Art Library.

page 111: Janet Fisher (1867–1926). Whitford & Hughes/Bridgeman Art Library.

pages 120–121: Jane Benham-Hay (1820–70). Russell-Cotes Art Gallery and Museum, Bournemouth, UK/Bridgeman Art Library.

Text Credits & References

page 29: Clarissa Pinkola Estès *Women Who Run With the Wolves*, Rider, 1992.

page 53, 103, 109: Robert Holden *Happiness Now!*, Hodder & Stoughton, 1999.

page 62: Dag Hammarskjöld (trans. W.H. Auden and Leif Sjoberg) *Markings* © 1964, Alfred A. Knopf, a division of Random House Inc. and Faber & Faber. Used with permission.

page 64: Robert Muller in *Decide to Forgive* by Maryann Hakowski and Kieran Sawyer and Ave Maria Press, 2001 © Ave Maria Press

page 90, 102: Foundation for Inner Peace *A Course in Miracles*, Arkana paperback, 1975.

page 95: Jack Kornfield *A Path With a Heart,* Rider,1993. Used by permission of The Random House Group Ltd.

page 122: Lewis Smedes 'Forgiveness: The Power to Change the Past' in *Christianity Today*, January 7, 1983.